"Many have died, Suzanna, but more will come.
There are always people who hope, who wish, who dream."

The Quick and the Dead, Louis L'Amour

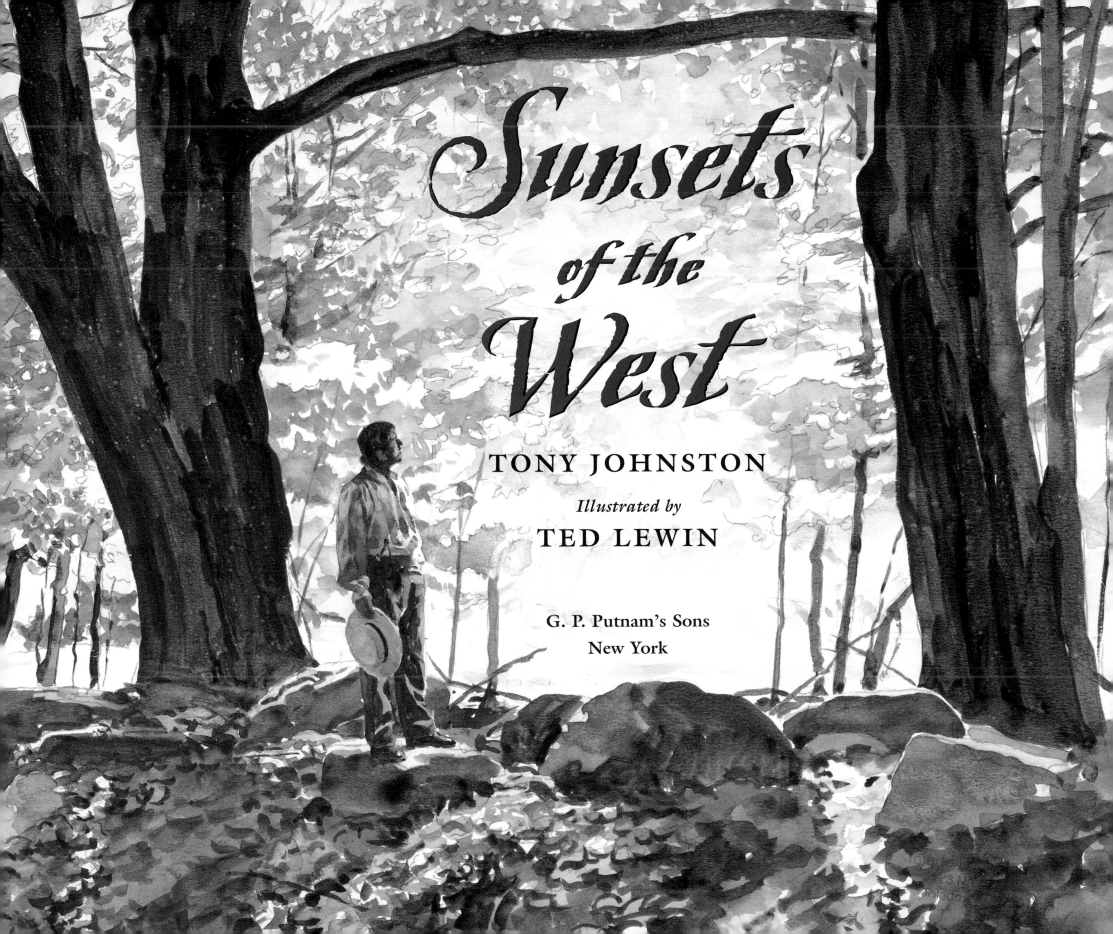

Sunsets
of the
West

TONY JOHNSTON

Illustrated by

TED LEWIN

G. P. Putnam's Sons
New York

Special thanks to Peter Blodgett, Curator of Western Historical Manuscripts, the Huntington Library, San Marino, California; to Philipsburg Manor, Historic Hudson Valley, for giving permission to Ted Lewin to photograph the oxen; and to the oxen's handlers, Steve Kozak and Peter Curtis. The oxen Ted Lewin used for his models are an old breed called line back cattle. Their names are Bright and Bold.

Designed by Cecilia Yung and Gunta Alexander. Text set in 15-point Galliard Bold. The art was done in watercolor.
Library of Congress Cataloging-in-Publication Data   Johnston, Tony.   Sunsets of the West / Tony Johnston ; illustrated by Ted Lewin.   p. cm.
Summary: Pa and his family pack up their belongings and undertake the difficult journey to a new life in the West. [1. Frontier and pioneer life—West (U.S.)—Fiction.]
I. Lewin, Ted, ill. II. Title. PZ7.J6478 Su 2002 [E]—dc21 00-066473   ISBN 0-399-22659-1   10 9 8 7 6 5 4 3 2 1   FIRST IMPRESSION

A NOTE TO THE READER

Using a covered wagon as their conveyance, a family would have taken one solid month (closer to two) to get from New England to Missouri, where wagon trains set out for the West. They must begin the trip from Missouri around mid-May, as soon as the worst of winter lets up. By then, the prairie grass would have been tall enough to feed the livestock. Should they start too early, grass could be sparse and the stock would starve. People dared not depart later than mid-June or too many wagons would have gone ahead, leaving little grass or forage. Each trip was a race with winter. If they dallied, they risked reaching the Sierra in late October when the first fierce snowstorms struck. All things in their favor, the entire trip would have lasted perhaps six or seven months.   —T. J.

In memory of Louis L'Amour,
whose books have entertained and enlightened me,
not once, but time and again.   —T. J.

To all the brave souls who made the journey.   —T. L.

ONCE a man felt a stirring in his heart, an itching to roam. And he felt pinched for space.

He knew the stars of Maine. He knew the blaze of fall leaves burning New Hampshire hills. Still, he longed to know the endless prairie. The Sierra with snow.

"Gather your necessaries," Pa said one day. "We're going West."

The family took pots and pans, spoons, forks, food, tools for farming. They took quilts that Ma had made. They took the cow. And the white chickens, lashed to their wagon in a coop. They lashed on barrels of water from the spring.

Ma said, "Gather your loved things."

So they took a book and dolls and seeds. Seeds that would sprout far away. Seeds to grow tall under Western sun.

When this was done, they turned toward their house.

"Good-bye," the youngest called. And they cried. Ma most of all. She was leaving behind her home.

Then they were gone. And the house stood silent, alone.

Walking beside the wagon, the children clucked like chickens about how things would be where they were going.

Inside it, there was not much room, so they'd strung spoons and pans from the wagon top. They'd slung the kettle from the bottom.

Pa "gee-upped" and "whoaed" the oxen.

Tink-tink, *tonk-tonk*, the necessaries clanked a metal song.
The ox bells clanked, *tonk-tonk*, *tink-tink*. The water sloshed in
the barrels. The wagon wheels creaked. Always they creaked as
the wagon rolled along.

The family joined other families going the same way.
At night they shared their campfire. Boys and girls,
mas and pas and babies, all under new stars. Fiddles
hummed like insect buzz. Tales buzzed too. They heard of
places called Devil's Hind Quarters, Adobe Walls, Wagon Mound.
Now Ma's heart felt new dreams pull. Now everyone itched to go on.

They heard new sounds. Wolves. Coyotes. Quail. Indians pretending to be quail. Sometimes, in the distance, they glimpsed them. They prayed the Indians would go their own way, for these were warriors, they were told. Warriors trying to hold their land.

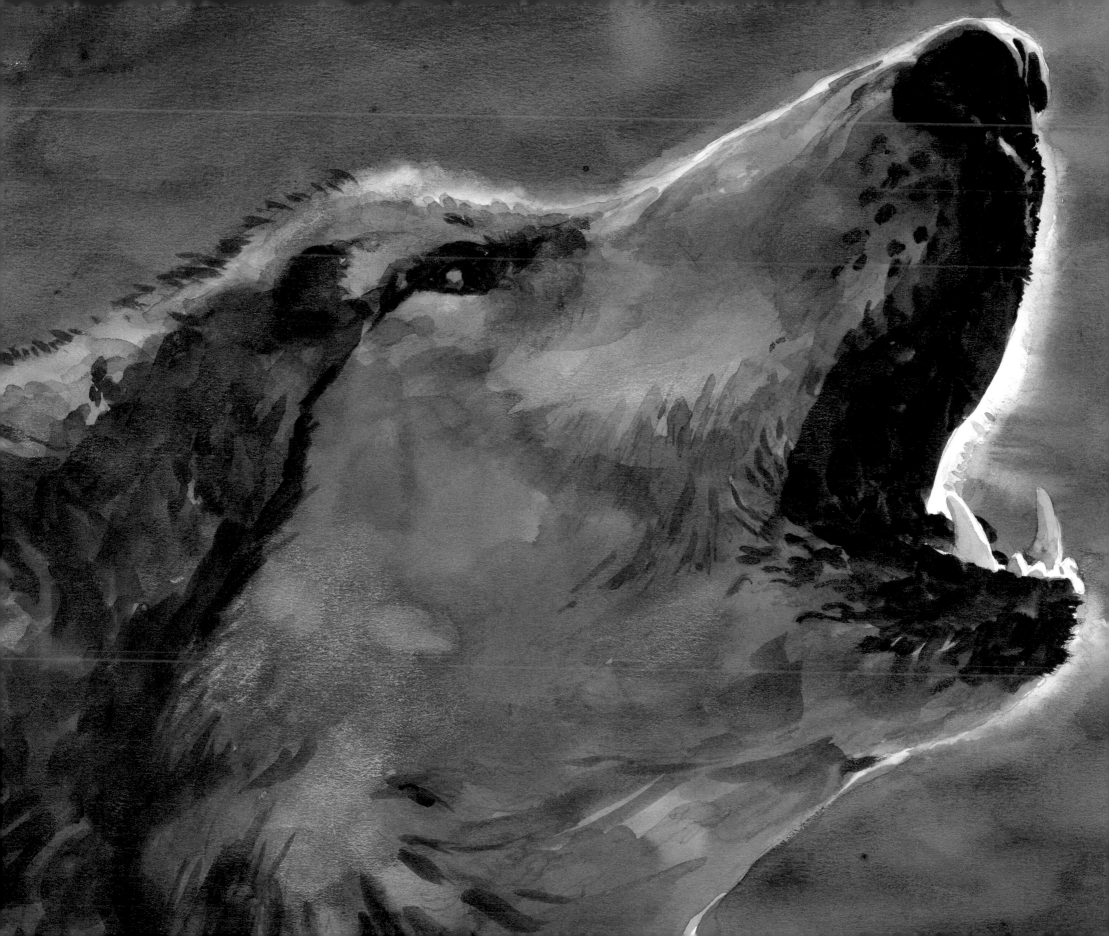

Sometimes the family knew the blaze of wagons
burning on the hills. People died. Then they cried.
And they went on.

When days got hot, everyone prayed for rain.
And bullet rain came down. Then Ma stuck the seeds
inside a biscuit tin to keep them dry.

When it rained, rivers swelled, first silver, then brown.
They churned up trees and washed everything away,
chickens and coop and cow.

Then the wagon creaked through mud. If a wheel broke, everyone helped fix it, while frogs sang in the mud.

The family sang like the frogs. Storm songs, wheel-fixing songs, songs for going on.

They came to the prairie, thick with flowers. There they saw great beasts chewing the flowers and the grass. Pa held back the wagon. And they waited, days sometimes, for the buffalo to pass.

They came to deserts of sunset sand. By day everything quivered with heat. Everything froze at night.

Ma checked the biscuit tin. Some seeds were shriveled, some still fat with life. She ran them through her hand, then back into the tin. Even the shriveled ones. She thought of her home far away. And she cried.

Every day they saw graves. And graves. And graves. And bones. Whenever they passed a marker, Pa slowed the wagon to honor the dead. The other wagons melted into the desert now, going their separate ways. Everyone sighed and said "luck to you." Everyone needed luck where they were bound.

Then the family was alone. And they went on.

The oxen got thirsty and tired. One of them lay down and died.

And the family cried. But they went on.

"Lighten the wagon, to move faster," Pa said.
So they sawed it in two. They threw away the loved
things and the necessaries. Everything that tinked
and tonked. But in her pocket, Ma kept the seeds.

Now they had no tears to cry. Now they sang
no song.

Other Indians came. Everyone grew still as stone.
The Indians brought food when they had none.
The family blessed them. And they went on.

One day they saw mountains washed with dawn. Mountains that stopped their breath.

They felt an itching to go up.

There, they heard wind shaking the trees. They smelled the pine-sharp air. They saw the sun sink, spilling its fire everywhere.

And everyone said, "We are here."

The family built a house and tilled a patch of land. Then they planted the seeds. And the seeds grew tall.

Sometimes they remembered the stars of Maine. Sometimes they recalled the blaze of fall leaves on New Hampshire hills. But they had seen the endless prairie. The Sierra with snow.

Their hearts were at rest. They knew the sunsets of the West.